PUFFIN BOOKS

Not Quite a Mermaid

MERMAID PROMISE

Linda Chapman lives in Leicestershire with
her family and a Bernese mountain dog.
When she is not writing she spends her time
looking after her young family, horse
riding and teaching drama.

Books by Linda Chapman

MY SECRET UNICORN series
NOT QUITE A MERMAID series
STARDUST series
UNICORN SCHOOL series

BRIGHT LIGHTS
CENTRE STAGE

Not Quite a Mermaid

MERMAID PROMISE

LINDA CHAPMAN

Illustrated by Dawn Apperley

PUFFIN

PUFFIN BOOKS

Published by the Penguin Group
Penguin Books Ltd, 80 Strand, London WC2R 0RL, England
Penguin Group (USA) Inc., 375 Hudson Street, New York, New York 10014, USA
Penguin Group (Canada), 90 Eglinton Avenue East, Suite 700, Toronto, Ontario,
Canada M4P 2Y3 (a division of Pearson Penguin Canada Inc.)
Penguin Ireland, 25 St Stephen's Green, Dublin 2, Ireland
(a division of Penguin Books Ltd)
Penguin Group (Australia), 250 Camberwell Road, Camberwell, Victoria 3124, Australia
(a division of Pearson Australia Group Pty Ltd)
Penguin Books India Pvt Ltd, 11 Community Centre, Panchsheel Park,
New Delhi – 110 017, India
Penguin Group (NZ), 67 Apollo Drive, Rosedale, North Shore 0632, New Zealand
(a division of Pearson New Zealand Ltd)
Penguin Books (South Africa) (Pty) Ltd, 24 Sturdee Avenue, Rosebank,
Johannesburg 2196, South Africa

Penguin Books Ltd, Registered Offices: 80 Strand, London WC2R 0RL, England

puffinbooks.com

First published 2008
1

Text copyright © Linda Chapman, 2008
Illustrations copyright © Dawn Apperley, 2008
All rights reserved

The moral right of the author and illustrator has been asserted

Set in Palatino 15/27 pt
Typeset by Palimpsest Book Production Limited, Grangemouth, Stirlingshire
Made and printed in England by Clays Ltd, St Ives plc

British Library Cataloguing in Publication Data
A CIP catalogue record for this book is available from the British Library

ISBN: 978–0–141–32232–2

www.greenpenguin.co.uk

Mixed Sources
Product group from well-managed
forests and other controlled sources
www.fsc.org Cert no. SA-COC-1592
© 1996 Forest Stewardship Council

Penguin Books is committed to a sustainable future
for our business, our readers and our planet.
The book in your hands is made from paper
certified by the Forest Stewardship Council.

To Amy

Contents

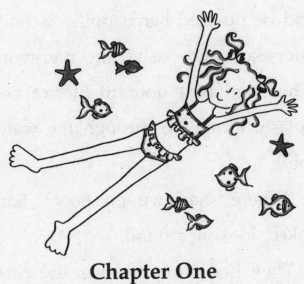

Chapter One

Electra the mermaid swam upwards and burst through the surface of the sea. As she shook the drops of water from her eyes, a dolphin popped up beside her. It was Splash, her best friend. Electra put her arm around him and he nuzzled her happily. Seconds later Sam and Sasha, the mer-twins who lived next door to Electra and Splash, swam up through the water too.

'Where shall we go now?' Sam asked, looking around.

They had surfaced near the coral wall that circled Mermaid Island – the

island where all the merpeople lived. Electra suddenly noticed something strange. 'The gates are open,' she pointed out. 'Look!'

In the coral wall there were two mother-of-pearl gates. Usually they were kept closed but just then they were open. The two mer-men on guard – Isa and Mellick – were looking out through them, waving and smiling.

'I wonder who Isa and Mellick are waving at,' said Sasha curiously.

'Let's go and see!' Electra exclaimed. She and Splash dived forward. The twins followed. As they reached the gates, Electra gasped. 'Oh, wow!'

Out in the deep sea, just beyond the reef, there was a group of about ten wild dolphins. They were leaping through the water.

'Bottlenose dolphins – like me!' whistled Splash.

Although a few porpoises – a kind of small dolphin – lived with the merpeople in the sea around Mermaid Island, there weren't any other bottlenose dolphins like Splash. Dolphins didn't usually stay in one place for long, but Splash was different.

Electra had found him stranded on a nearby island. His parents had been killed by sharks. He was too young to survive by himself and so he had come to live with Electra and her mum, Maris.

'They look as if they're having fun!' said Sam, grinning as two of the dolphins jumped over each other and the other dolphins all clapped their flippers.

Isa and Mellick looked round.

'Hi, you lot,' said Isa. 'Have you come to see the dolphins? They arrived about an hour ago. They're very friendly and I think they're going to stay around here for a few days.'

'Can I go and say hello?' Splash asked eagerly.

Usually the merpeople and their friends stayed out of the deep sea because dangerous creatures like sharks and electric eels sometimes lurked there. But Isa nodded. 'You can,

Splash. The sea's safe today. There have been no shark sightings this week.'

Splash sped like a grey arrow through the water towards the other dolphins.

'I bet it'll be fun for him saying hi to them,' said Sam.

Electra nodded enviously. She would have liked to go too, but she knew it was too late to catch up with Splash now. She was the slowest swimmer on Mermaid Island because she had two legs instead of a tail like all the other merpeople. This was

because she had been born a human.
The merpeople had found her floating
in a boat after a storm when she was
just a baby. They had decided to look
after her and had given her sea powder
so she could breathe underwater.
Maris, a young mermaid without any
children, had adopted her. Electra
didn't mind being different from the

other merpeople – having legs could be quite useful at times – but she often wished she could swim faster.

'It must be strange for Splash never seeing any other dolphins like him,' said Sam.

Electra nodded. Splash had reached the other dolphins. Some of them were diving around him and others were nuzzling him.

'How long has Splash been living here now?' Sasha asked Electra. 'It must be about a year.'

'Almost exactly,' Electra replied, watching Splash as he jumped into the air in excitement. 'I found him on Craggy Island a year ago this Friday.'

'You should have a party or something to celebrate him having been here for a year,' suggested Sam.

Electra stared at him. 'That's a brilliant idea, Sam! We could make it a surprise party and invite everyone who knows him.'

'We could all give Splash presents,' said Sasha. 'He would love it!'

'Oh, yes!' Electra exclaimed in delight. 'I'll ask Mum.'

'Why don't you swim back to your cave and ask her now,' suggested Sam. He glanced out to sea. 'Splash looks like he's going to be out there for quite a while. Sasha and I can wait here and if he does get back before you do, we'll just say you popped home but will be back in a minute.'

'OK,' said Electra. 'I'll be back as soon as I can!'

Electra raced to the cave she lived in with her mum and Splash. She found her mum in the kitchen, chatting to Ronan, the twins' dad.

'Mum! Mum! Sam, Sasha and I have had a brilliant idea!' Electra exclaimed.

'What is it?' her mum asked, looking interested.

'We think we should have a surprise party for Splash!' Electra burst out. 'It's a year on Friday since he came to live with us!'

To her delight, her mum smiled immediately. 'I think that's a great idea. We haven't ever had a birthday party for him because we don't know when his birthday is. This celebration could be a kind of belated birthday party. We could have it here, at home.'

'I'll help with the food,' offered Ronan.

'Sam, Sasha and I can make some decorations and write the invitations,' said Electra. 'It could be on Friday morning.'

Her mum nodded. 'OK. I'll start organizing it right away.'

'I'll go and tell Sam and Sasha,' said Electra.

She dived back out of the cave, excitement buzzing through her. A surprise party for Splash! She couldn't wait!

Chapter Two

'Well? What did your mum say?' Sam demanded when Electra returned.

'She said yes!' Electra exclaimed. 'We can have the party! I said you'd help me do the decorations and invitations.'

'Of course we will,' said Sasha. 'And I'll make Splash a shell necklace as a present.'

'I'll make him some starfish-shaped biscuits,' said Sam. 'What present will you get him, Electra?'

'Well . . .' Electra had been thinking about that very thing on the swim back to the gates. 'I think I'm going to make him a den.'

The twins looked puzzled. 'A den?' echoed Sasha.

'Splash doesn't have a bedroom of his own,' Electra explained. 'He sleeps on the floor of my cave, and I think he would really like a den. I'm going to find a cave and decorate it and make it into his own special place.'

Sasha smiled. 'That's a great idea! I bet he'll love it!'

'Sssh! I can see him coming back.' Sam pointed to where Splash's grey fin could be seen whizzing through the water.

'Don't say a word about the

party,' Electra warned. 'Or about his presents.'

Splash popped up beside them.

'Hi, Splash. Did you have fun?' Electra asked. She could feel a grin pulling at the corners of her mouth. It was really hard to act normally. She was longing to tell him about the party.

'It was brilliant!' Splash's dark eyes sparkled. 'The wild dolphins have seen some amazing things. They told me about watching turtles laying their eggs, and swimming with sea cows, and visiting islands with all sorts of

strange birds and monkeys. I'm going
to ask your mum if I can go and see
them every day while they're here.'

'I want to come and meet them too,'
said Electra. She looked at the twins.
'What about you?'

They shook their heads. 'I'm not

going out in the deep sea,' said Sasha. Like most of the merpeople she and Sam didn't like doing anything adventurous. Electra was different. She loved having adventures. Luckily Splash did too! They'd done some really exciting things together, like finding treasure, camping, talking to giant squid and escaping from sharks.

'What shall we do now?' Splash asked, looking round.

'Why don't we go and play hide and seek in the deep caves?' Electra suggested.

'OK,' Splash said eagerly.

He dived into the sea and they all raced after him.

To Electra's delight, while they were playing hide and seek, she discovered the perfect cave for Splash's secret den. Its entrance was hidden behind an overhanging rock so it was very private. It had ledges on the walls that could be used for shelves and two big rocks on the floor that looked like seats. Electra imagined it with a seaweed rug on the floor and with shells and pictures on the walls.

She whispered about it to Sam and Sasha while they were hiding from Splash.

'It sounds perfect!' Sasha whispered back. 'Let's come back tomorrow afternoon and start decorating it.'

That evening, Splash told Maris all about the wild dolphins. 'It was brilliant!' he said. 'Can I go and visit them tomorrow?'

'Me too?' asked Electra.

'All right,' Maris told them. 'So long

as there have been no shark sightings you can both go out tomorrow morning.'

Electra looked happily at Splash. A morning playing with the wild dolphins! That was going to be so much fun!

When Splash and Electra swam out of the gates the next day, the wild dolphins raced over to meet them. Their sleek grey bodies gleamed in the water. 'Hello, Splash!' they called.

'Hi!' he replied. 'This is Electra. I told you about her yesterday – she's my best friend!'

'Hello,' Electra said. The dolphins nosed around her, touching her arms and legs.

'I'm Flicker,' said one of them. 'Do you want to play tag with us, Electra?'

Electra nodded. 'Yeah!' She set off but the dolphins were so fast that they caught her easily.

'Hold on to me, Electra,' Splash offered. 'I'll pull you through the water and then you'll go faster.'

She grabbed hold of his fin but it slowed Splash down so much the other dolphins started catching him easily too.

'It's OK, Splash. I'll just watch,'

Electra told him, not minding at all. Swimming a little way off, she watched as Splash carried on playing. Without her holding on to him, he was just as fast as the others. He ducked and dived and leapt through the water, whistling with delight. She smiled. He looked so happy.

When they finally stopped racing around, the dolphins told stories about some of the amazing things they'd seen. They told Electra and Splash about how they had visited sunken ships with treasure on board, seen a group of sea dragons, swum with huge whales and passed an island with monkeys hanging from every tree. It sounded very exciting!

When Electra and Splash got home for lunch, Maris wanted to know all about their morning.

'We played tag,' Splash said. 'The wild dolphins are very fast but I could keep up with them, couldn't I, Electra?'

She nodded. 'You were really good. My favourite bit of the morning was when they told us about all the places they've been to.'

'I wish I could be a wild dolphin,'

said Splash longingly. 'I'd love to have
had all those adventures.'

Maris looked at him. 'Would you
really like to be a wild dolphin?'

'Oh, yes!' whistled Splash. 'It would
be brilliant to travel through the sea.'

'Me too,' agreed Electra. 'Wouldn't

you like to go travelling, Mum?' She knew her mum was quite adventurous for a mermaid.

'Maybe a bit, but I really like living on Mermaid Island,' Maris replied. 'We're merpeople, it's our home.' She glanced at Splash and her eyes seemed troubled. Electra had the sudden

feeling that there was something on her mind.

'Can I go back and see the dolphins again this afternoon, Maris?' Splash asked eagerly.

Maris nodded. 'Of course you can. You hardly ever get to see other dolphins. It's no wonder you want to be with them.'

'Are you going to come with me, Electra?' Splash asked.

Electra remembered the plans she'd made with Sam and Sasha for decorating the cave. 'No. I won't. I've got stuff to do.'

'What sort of stuff?' Splash asked curiously.

'Oh, just stuff with Sam and Sasha.' Electra shrugged, trying to pretend it was no big deal. 'I'll see you at tea time though. Have a good time with the wild dolphins!'

He whizzed round the cave in excitement. 'I will!'

Chapter Three

Electra, Sam and Sasha worked on
Splash's den all afternoon. They made
a rug by plaiting fronds of purple
seaweed together and found two big
blue sea sponges and put them on the
rocks to sit on. Then Electra made a

notice that she hung inside the entrance. It said in big black writing: *Splash's Den*. They all drew some pictures for Splash and hung them round the walls.

'That'll do for today,' said Electra, pleased with all they had done. 'We should go and write the invitations for the party.'

'Let's do them in our cave,' said Sasha. 'We don't want Splash to see.'

Electra had just put the last invitation in an envelope when she heard Splash calling her name outside. Leaving Sam and Sasha to hide the invitations in case Splash came in and saw them, she swam out of their cave. 'Hi,' she called.

'Hi,' said Splash quietly.

He was looking upset. 'What's the matter?' Electra asked.

'Flicker and the others have just told me that they are going to be leaving the island on Friday – the day after tomorrow,' Splash replied.

'Oh, Splash,' Electra said. 'You'll really miss them, won't you?'

Splash nodded. Electra wished she could tell him about the party to cheer him up.

Just then, Maris came out of their cave. 'Hello, Splash. Have you had a good afternoon?'

'Yes, but the dolphins are moving on soon. I'm going to have to say goodbye to them.' He looked dejected. 'It's so much fun playing with other dolphins like me.'

'You're growing up, Splash,' Maris said slowly. 'You know, maybe –' She

broke off as if she had changed her mind about what she'd been about to say.

'Maybe what?' Splash asked curiously.

Maris cleared her throat. 'It . . . it doesn't matter. I'd better go and check on tea.'

She went back into the cave quickly. Electra wondered what her mum had been about to say. She thought about it for a few seconds and then pushed the thought to the back of her mind. She had more important things to think about – like getting everything ready for Splash's party!

After Splash had gone to see the dolphins the next morning, Electra began to make some decorations for the party they were going to have at home. Maris swam in just as she had got started. 'Electra, we need to talk.'

'About the party?' Electra didn't wait for her mum to answer. 'I'm really glad we're having it. I hope it cheers Splash up after the wild dolphins have gone.'

'That's what I want to talk to you about.' Maris sighed. 'He doesn't have to say goodbye to them.'

Electra frowned. 'What? Of course he's got to say goodbye. They're moving on.'

'What I mean is . . . well, he wouldn't have to say goodbye if he went with them,' Maris explained.

Electra stared at her. 'What?'

Maris swam over and took her hands. 'Oh, Electra, I've been thinking about this all night. Splash has been very happy here with us for the last year – playing with you, living in our cave. But he's growing up now and maybe . . .' Maris bit her lip. 'Maybe now he's getting older, he needs other things. Mermaid Island is our home because we're merpeople. But Splash isn't a merperson, he's a dolphin, and perhaps his place is out in the deep sea with the other dolphins. He's been so happy playing with them the last few days. Perhaps we should see if he wants to go with them.'

'No,' Electra whispered, her heart pounding.

Her mum looked torn and unhappy. 'I really don't want him to go either, but there's a saying: if you love someone, set them free. It means that if you love someone you should do what is needed to make them happy. If it would make Splash happiest to be with the other dolphins, then we should let him go.'

'But it wouldn't make him happy!' The words burst out of Electra. 'He wouldn't like it!'

'You mean *you* wouldn't like it,' her mum said gently. She squeezed Electra's

hands. 'Maybe we should ask Splash what *he* wants.'

Electra stared at her.

'We have to give him the choice, Electra. Look, I'll talk to him . . .' Maris began.

'No, Mum,' Electra said quickly. The last thing she wanted was her mum *persuading* Splash to leave.

'Well, then you must promise me that you will,' Maris said.

Electra hesitated and then nodded. 'OK, I promise,' she muttered.

Maris hugged her. 'Good girl. I'll see you later and we can talk then.'

She swam away.

Electra sank down on her bed. She thought about the way Splash's eyes sparkled when he talked about the wild dolphins' adventures and about how much he loved playing with them. Maybe he *would* be happier living with them.

But then she shook her head. Whatever her mum said, she knew Splash would be happier with her on Mermaid Island. *I can't let him go*, she thought fiercely. *I won't!*

Chapter Four

Splash raced into Electra's room when he got back later that morning. 'Oh, Electra, I've had a brilliant time! It was great, we . . .'

But Electra didn't want to hear about how much fun he'd been having with the dolphins. 'I've had an idea!' she interrupted, jumping to her feet. 'Why don't we go to Turtle Rock and play hide and seek?' Playing in the waters around Turtle Rock was one of Splash's favourite things to do.

'OK,' Splash said eagerly.

Electra felt a flutter of relief. Maybe if they did all the things he really liked doing he'd stop thinking about how much fun it was being with the other dolphins and think about the great time he had with her on Mermaid Island instead.

They swam to Turtle Rock and began to play hide and seek.

'Found you!' whistled Splash as he found Electra hiding behind a giant clam.

Electra grinned. 'This is fun, isn't it?'

'Yes, and I had loads more fun with the other dolphins this morning too,'

Splash said happily. 'I love hearing their stories.'

'I can tell you stories,' said Electra. 'Once upon a time there was a sea fairy and –'

'Don't be silly! That's just a made-up story, Electra,' Splash said, bumping her with his nose. 'The wild dolphins tell stories about *real* adventures, not pretend ones.'

Electra felt hurt. Splash had always liked her stories before.

'We all played tag again as well,' said Splash.

'We can do that!' Electra said quickly.

'Come on!' She tagged him and dashed away. 'You're it!'

Splash caught her easily.

'Got you!' he whistled. 'You're so easy to catch – much easier than the other dolphins. Try and get me.'

But, hard as Electra tried, she

couldn't. She felt herself swimming slower and slower as he swam away from her. Tears prickled in her eyes. She would never be as good as the wild dolphins, never be as much fun as them. Maybe her mum was right. Maybe Splash really should go with them.

Splash swam back to her in surprise. 'Why aren't you trying to catch me any more?'

'I don't feel like it,' she muttered.

He pushed her arm with his nose. 'You're sad. What's the matter?'

She didn't say anything.

'Electra?' Splash said anxiously. 'What is it?'

She put her arms round him. 'I'm OK,' she said, burying her head in his neck and swallowing hard. 'I . . . I love you, Splash. I really do.'

'I know that. I love you too,' he said, sounding confused.

Electra hugged him tightly.

She heard her mum's voice in her mind: *if you love someone, set them free.*

She knew that now was the moment when she should ask Splash if he wanted to leave Mermaid Island and go with the other dolphins. But she just couldn't bring herself to. What if he said yes?

I can't do it, she thought desperately. *I just can't.*

'Electra?' Splash said, his voice muffled by her arms. 'What's wrong?'

'Nothing,' she lied. She pushed all

thoughts of asking him out of her mind. 'Come on, let's go home.'

Electra didn't sleep well that night. When she got up, much earlier than normal, Maris was in the kitchen. 'Did you talk to Splash yesterday?' she asked Electra.

Electra shook her head.

'Oh, Electra,' her mum said, swimming over to her. 'I know it's hard. I don't want Splash to go with the other dolphins either, but we have to let him decide for himself. If you won't ask him then I will.'

'No, I'll do it, Mum,' Electra said quickly. 'I promise.'

She swam out of the kitchen before her mum could say anything more.

When Splash got up he looked sad and his flippers drooped. 'I don't want any breakfast,' he told Maris quietly. 'I'm going to go and say goodbye to my friends. They said they'd be leaving early.'

Maris exchanged looks with Electra. Electra's heart sank. She guessed she couldn't put off talking to him any longer.

'I'll swim to the reef wall with you,' she said.

They set off. Splash sighed. 'I can't believe I've got to say goodbye to them. I'll miss them so much.'

Electra took a deep breath. 'Maybe you *don't* have to say goodbye.'

Splash frowned. 'What do you mean?'

'You . . . you could go with them if you wanted,' Electra whispered. The words felt like they were hurting her throat.

He looked puzzled. 'Go with them?'

Electra swallowed hard. 'Yes, you could go and be a wild dolphin.'

'But that would mean leaving you,' Splash said slowly.

Electra nodded.

Splash stared at her. 'Don't be silly. I don't want to leave you, Electra.'

'But you really like being with the other dolphins. You've said how much you would love to be like them and you've been really unhappy at the thought of saying goodbye. Maybe you should go, Splash. I . . . I don't mind,' she lied.

Splash looked confused. 'Wouldn't you miss me if I went then?'

'Of course I would!' The words

burst out of Electra. This was the hardest thing she'd ever done. Harder than stopping sharks attacking the merpeople, harder than stopping a shoal of starfish eating the coral reef. Every bit of her wanted to beg Splash not to go, to tell him that she would be really unhappy, but, once again, her mum's words ran round in her head: *if you love someone, set them free*. She *did* love Splash and she wanted him to be happy even if that meant she had to say goodbye to him. She took a deep breath and tried to sound calmer. 'Of course I'd miss you, Splash, but I've got other friends. I'll . . . I'll be all right.'

'Oh.' Splash's fins suddenly seemed to droop more.

'If you want to go, you really should,' Electra told him.

Splash didn't seem to know what to say.

Electra felt a sob rise up inside her. He really was thinking about going! She turned and dived away. She didn't want him to see her cry. *I want him to be happy*, she told herself over and over again.

'Electra!' Splash whistled desperately.

She glanced round. He was looking confused and upset.

'I've got to go,' he said, turning. 'But –'

'You're going?' she interrupted.

'Yes, they're about to leave and I need to –'

Electra couldn't bear it. She dived

61

away, cutting him off before he could say any more. When she next looked round, there was just empty sea.

Splash had gone!

Chapter Five

Electra burst into tears. Seeing the cave that she had made for his den, she swam inside. It was just as she and the twins had left it the day before, the rug on the floor, the pictures on the walls, and the notice that said *Splash's Den*.

Sitting on the rug, Electra wrapped her arms around her knees and sobbed. Splash had left her. He really had gone and he hadn't even said a proper goodbye.

Suddenly Sam and Sasha's voices floated through the water towards her. 'I wonder if Electra's here.'

'I can't wait for the party.'

Electra froze. The party! Oh, no! She'd forgotten all about it. It was that morning. What was she going to say to everyone?

The twins swam round the rock and into the cave. They were both carrying streamers made of pink and purple seaweed. 'Oh, hi, Electra,' Sam said, looking surprised to see her sitting on the floor.

'H-hi,' she stammered, jumping to her feet.

'We thought we'd come and put up a few decorations in here as well,' Sam said. 'Is Splash with the dolphins again?'

Electra couldn't bring herself to say that Splash had gone. She nodded wordlessly.

'I can't wait until he gets back,' Sasha said. 'He's going to love his party!'

'And this cave!' said Sam. 'Let's get these decorations up.'

'I . . . I don't feel very well,' Electra mumbled. 'I think I might go home.'

'Are you OK?' said Sasha in concern. 'Should I come with you?'

Electra shook her head. 'I . . . I'm

fine.' She swam out of the den. Memories of Splash flashed into her mind – Splash when she'd first seen him on the beach on Craggy Island, Splash playing jokes with her, Splash and her talking to a giant Napoleon fish, Splash's mischievous dark eyes sparkling at her . . .

She reached their cave. She couldn't
face going in and telling her mum that
the party was off – that Splash had
gone. She sat down on a rock outside.
I can't bear it, she thought desperately.
I really can't bear it.

Misery overwhelmed her and,
burying her head in her arms, she
began to sob as if her heart was
breaking.

Suddenly someone nudged her arm.
She looked up – and gasped. Splash
was swimming in the water next to
her.

'Splash!' Electra exclaimed.

'What's the matter?' he asked. 'Why are you crying, Electra?'

'I thought you'd gone.' Electra could hardly believe he was there in front of her. She put out a hand and touched him. 'I thought you'd left to be with the dolphins.'

'No,' Splash said. 'I just went to say

goodbye to them. I had to because they were about to go.' He looked sad. 'I know it doesn't matter to you very much if I stay or not,' he muttered. 'But I want to stay. You're my best friend. I don't want to go anywhere without you.'

'Oh, Splash!' Happiness rushed through Electra. 'You're my best friend too! I'm so glad you're not going!'

Splash looked confused. 'But you said you wouldn't mind if I went.'

'I didn't *mean* it! I just didn't want you to stay if you would really be happier with the dolphins.' Electra threw her arms round him. 'I hated the thought you might leave!'

'And I hated the thought of going,' Splash whistled. 'I know the wild dolphins have fun but I wouldn't have enjoyed being with them. I would have been too unhappy without you.'

Electra felt relief roll over her. She hugged him as tightly as she could. 'Don't ever go away, Splash.'

'Never ever,' he promised, nuzzling her hair.

Electra hugged him and then broke free as she suddenly remembered the party. She had to get Splash out of the way or it wouldn't be a surprise! 'Come on, why don't we play for a bit? We can celebrate you not going.'

'OK,' Splash said.

'I'll just tell Mum. You stay here!'

Electra popped in through the shell curtain. Maris was in the lounge. 'Electra, have you asked Splash about the dolphins?' she asked.

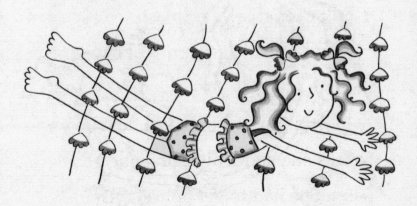

'Yes, but he doesn't want to! He's staying!' Electra grabbed her mum's hands and swung her round. 'He's staying! He's staying! He's staying!'

Maris looked very relieved. 'Oh, I'm so glad! I didn't think he would leave but I just felt we had to give him the

choice.' She kissed Electra. 'I'm proud of you for asking.'

Electra felt so happy she swam a loop-the-loop. She glanced round. 'I'd better go. He's just outside.'

'Bring him back here just after eleven,' Maris said. She smiled. 'We don't want Splash to be late for his own party!'

Electra grinned back. 'I'll bring him back on time! I promise!' And with that she dived out of the cave.

Chapter Six

Electra and Splash played hide and seek with Electra keeping a careful eye on the time. Just before eleven o'clock they headed home. When they got there Electra hung back and let Splash swim into the cave first.

'*Surprise!*' all the guests yelled as they popped out from behind the sofa and chairs and out of the doorways. They were all wearing party hats and throwing streamers. Splash stopped in astonishment.

'Happy birthday, Splash.' Maris swam forward with a birthday hat and put it on his head.

'A birthday party? For me!' Splash said as Electra joined him.

Maris kissed him. 'Yes, for you. We realized that you hadn't had a birthday since you got here so we decided to celebrate today – a whole year since you came to live with us.'

Everyone crowded round and handed him present after present. Splash looked as if he couldn't believe his eyes. 'A new blanket! A chest of sweets. A shell necklace,' he said. 'Thank you, everyone!'

When everyone had given him their presents they all began to eat.

There were sandwiches, cakes with different-coloured icing, strands of sugar seaweed, shells made out of candy, wobbly red jellyfish jellies and a huge birthday cake with a dolphin on top. After a while, Maris put some music on and people started to dance.

Electra and Splash sat together.

Electra sighed happily. 'Are you enjoying yourself, Splash?'

'Oh, yes,' he said, watching as Sam and Sasha danced and all their other friends and the grown-ups joined in too. 'I think this is the best day of my life.'

'And mine,' said Electra. She put her arm around him. 'And to think I

thought it was going to be the worst.'
She remembered the den. Everyone
was having so much fun dancing they
wouldn't miss her and Splash for a
little while. 'I've got a surprise for
you.'

'Another one!' Splash said in
astonishment.

Electra nodded. 'My own special
one.' She swam out of the cave. 'Come
on!'

As Electra showed him into the den,
Splash looked around in astonishment.
'Where are we?'

Electra pointed at the notice.

'*Splash's Den,*' Splash read out. His eyes widened in wonder as he took in the cushions, the pictures, the rug, the seaweed streamers the twins had put up, the tin of biscuits. 'This is all for me?'

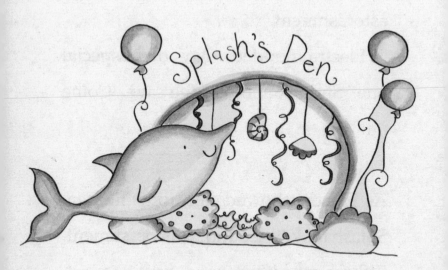

Electra nodded. 'It's your own special place. The twins helped me to get it ready. Do you like it?'

'I love it!' gasped Splash. 'Thank you, Electra! This is the best present ever.' He nuzzled her. 'And you're the best friend ever.'

She was delighted.

'I can't believe you thought I'd really want to leave you,' Splash said.

'I didn't, it was just that Mum said now you were growing up you might need different things,' Electra explained. 'She thought that you might not be happy here on Mermaid

Island with us – I wanted you to be happy.'

'But I couldn't be happy without you, Electra,' protested Splash. 'I'm never going to leave you. I'm going to be your dolphin for life.' He clapped his flippers. 'Your life dolphin!'

Electra grinned. 'And I'll be your life mermaid.'

Splash whistled happily. 'We'll live on Mermaid Island forever – having adventures!'

'Lots and lots of adventures,' Electra agreed. 'I want us to go out looking for a sea witch and to find a sea dragon.'

'And I want us to go swimming

with some giant rays,' said Splash. 'And meet a sea cow.'

'There are so many exciting things for us to do!' Electra said happily.

'And the best thing is we're going to be doing them together,' Splash declared.

Electra kissed his nose. 'Forever,' she smiled.

Discover magical new worlds with
Linda Chapman

✭ **Gallop** with the unicorns at Unicorn Meadows

✭ **Fly** with the magical spirits of Stardust Forest

✭ **Swim** through Mermaid Falls with Electra and her friends

✭ **Play** with new friends at Unicorn School

With great **activities**, gorgeous **downloads**, games galore and an exciting new online fanzine!

What are you waiting for?
The magic begins at

lindachapman.co.uk